Rani's Sea Spell

Gwyneth Rees is half Welsh and half English and grew up in Scotland. She went to Glasgow University and qualified as a doctor in 1990. She is a child and adolescent psychiatrist, but has now stopped practising so that she can write full-time.

She is the author of many bestselling books, including the Fairies series, the Mermaid series, the Magic Princess Dress series, the My Super Sister series and the Cosmo series, as well as several books for older readers. She lives near London with her husband, Robert, and their daughters, Eliza and Lottie.

Books by Gwyneth Rees

Mermaid Magic
Rani's Sea Spell
The Shell Princess

Fairy Dust
Fairy Treasure
Fairy Dreams
Fairy Gold
Fairy Rescue
Fairy Secrets

Cosmo and the Magic Sneeze
Cosmo and the Great Witch Escape
Cosmo and the Secret Spell

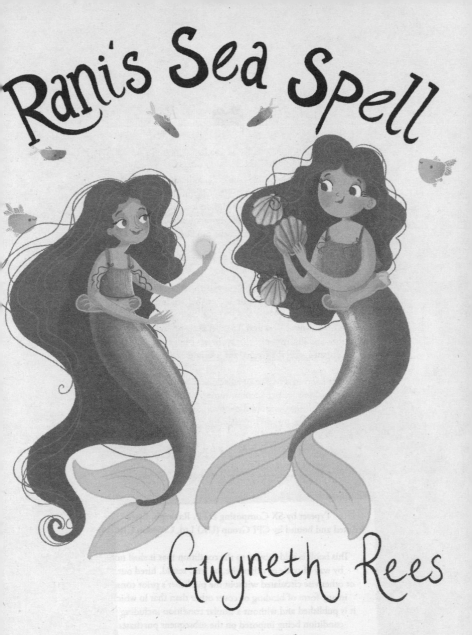

Rani's Sea Spell

Gwyneth Rees

Illustrated by Annabel Hudson

MACMILLAN CHILDREN'S BOOKS

First published 2001 by Macmillan Children's Books

This edition published 2016 by Macmillan Children's Books
an imprint of Pan Macmillan
20 New Wharf Road, London N1 9RR
Associated companies throughout the world
www.panmacmillan.com

ISBN 978-1-5098-1870-9

1 3 5 7 9 8 6 4 2

A CIP catalogue record for this book is available from
the British Library.

For Rani and Sunil

Rani and her family were having breakfast. The water in their cave was lovely and warm because the hot-rock stove was on and Roscoe, Rani's pet sea horse, was floating lazily next to it.

They all jumped as a huge fishy nose pushed itself through the seaweed-flap that covered the cave entrance.

"It's Pat!" Rani and her sister, Kai, left their breakfast and swam over to greet the big grey dolphin who was now half in and half out of the cave. Pat brought them messages from outside Tingle Reef.

"Is everything all right?" asked their mother, who was sitting on the seaweed mat feeding their baby sister, Pearl, with a tiny shell-spoon.

"Everything is fine," Pat reassured her. "I've brought you an invitation. Your mother wants you all to visit them next week. They're throwing a grand party!"

Rani's grandmother didn't live in Tingle Reef. She lived inside a shipwreck in the Deep Blue. Rani's mother had lived there when she was a child and had told them lots of exciting stories about it.

"A party!" shouted Kai. "Oh, please can we go, Mother?"

Rani and Kai had never been to their grandmother's home before. You had to swim far into the Deep Blue to get there and, until now, their parents had always said that they were too young to make the trip.

"Well . . ." Miriam looked at her husband, clearly excited by the idea of the party as well. "What do you think, Murdoch?"

Their father looked thoughtful. "I think Kai and Rani probably *are* old enough to go this time, but we should get someone to look after Pearl."

"*YES!*" shouted Rani and Kai together, clasping hands and swishing their tails in unison as they propelled themselves excitedly round the cave.

"Come in and have some breakfast with us, Pat," Murdoch said, but the

dolphin replied that he had several more
messages to deliver.

"But I'll tell them to expect you at the
party!" he said, giving them his biggest
dolphin grin as he backed out of the
cave.

Rani couldn't wait to tell her friend,
Morva, about the party. Morva was

known in Tingle Reef as the sea-witch because she was very old and wise and she could do magic. Morva's magic was always good – but some of the other mermaids were afraid of her. She lived in a special floating cave in the Deep Blue, just outside Tingle Reef, and Rani often went to visit her there.

Rani and Morva weren't like the other mermaids. Instead of having blonde hair and green tails like the others, they had red hair and orange tails. Morva's hair was so long that it touched the tip of her tail. And even though she was very old – almost ancient – Morva still looked young and beautiful.

There was a special reason why Rani was such a frequent visitor to Morva's cave – a reason that most of the other mermaids didn't know about. Rani had recently discovered that she too had magic powers, and now Morva was teaching her how to make them stronger.

As Rani swam out through the Deep Blue towards Morva's floating cave, all she could think about was the party and what she was going to wear. She had some special shell-combs which she could put in her hair and some glitter-sand to make her hair sparkly . . .

Rani found the cave floating in its usual place, past the bushy sea-cactus with the blue flowers and straight up from the needle-shaped bush. She swam through the opening in the magic rock, grabbed hold of the seaweed rope and hauled herself up the narrow vertical tunnel that led inside.

"Wow!" she gasped, as she entered Morva's cave. The water inside the floating cave was usually crystal clear, but today Morva had changed the colour to pink with one of her sea-spells.

Morva beckoned for Rani to come and join her. Although Morva's face was young and beautiful, her eyes were old and wise. She was sitting on a rock with her long red hair billowing out around her as she listened to two lobsters playing a duet on some shell-horns. When they had finished, Rani joined in Morva's clapping.

"I taught them that melody myself," Morva said. "Now, Rani . . . Let's see

what I can teach *you* today."

Neither Morva or Rani had been born in Tingle Reef. Rani had been found as a baby and adopted by Miriam and Murdoch. They had found her inside a Giant Clam-Shell on the edge of the reef and nobody knew how she had got there. Morva had come to Tingle Reef long before Rani's parents – or

even her grandparents – had been born.
She came from a community of magic
mermaids who lived in a secret place
far away and Morva had promised
that one day she would take Rani there –
but first Rani had to learn a lot more
magic.

Before Rani had time to tell her about
the party, Morva was swimming about
the cave looking for something. "We
need something to mend. Aah! This will
do." She lifted up a delicate shell-dish
and banged it against the cave wall so
that it broke into several pieces. "Right,"
said Morva briskly. "What have I told
you about starting up magic?"

"You have to *think* it up inside your
head," said Rani, as she desperately tried

to stop thinking about glitter-sand and shell-combs.

"Exactly. Which means you have to concentrate very hard indeed, so close your eyes . . ."

Rani closed her eyes and tried to focus on the mending spell but all she could think about was her grandmother's party.

Morva peered at her more closely. "You're very excited about something. What is it?"

And at last Rani was able to tell her about the dolphin's visit that morning.

"Well, that *is* exciting," replied Morva. "Now let me think . . ." She looked thoughtful. "I know! I will give you a special sea-spell to take with you on your journey."

"What sort of spell?" asked Rani eagerly. "What does it do?"

"Before I tell you that," Morva said, "I need to be sure that you can concentrate hard enough to make the spell work."

"Of course I can!" Rani burst out. To prove it, she closed her eyes and started to concentrate again on the mending spell, picturing the broken pieces of shell-dish coming back together again. She could feel a tingling sensation starting up in her belly button and spreading upwards. Soon her fingertips felt warm. She opened her eyes and saw that they were glowing. Slowly, she spread out her fingers above the broken pieces of shell.

"Well done!" Morva smiled.

The shell-dish was all in one piece again, surrounded by a golden glow.

Rani grinned. "I did it!"

Morva nodded, still smiling. "Now, let me tell you about my special sea-spell . . ."

chapter Two

On the morning they were due to set off
for the shipwreck, Rani and her family
got up very early indeed. The shipwreck
was a long way away and it would take
them most of the day to get there.

As they got ready, there was a knock at
the door of their cave.

"That will be Morva," their mother
said. Morva had offered to look after
Pearl while they were gone.

"Come in!" everyone shouted, and
Morva swam inside the cave, her red

hair streaming out behind her.

"Octavius is here too," Morva said.

Octavius, the octopus, followed her into the cave. He had tied two of his long wriggly arms together to make a loop and hanging from the loop were lots of shell-containers and bulky seaweed bags.

"Pat told me about the party and I'm

coming too. My sister, Flora, lives on the shipwreck," Octavius explained. "I can't think why she didn't send me an invitation!"

"Why are you taking so much stuff?" asked Kai.

"Ah, well . . . That's the trouble with having a huge brain like mine – one thinks of so many things to pack." He sighed as he readjusted some of his bags.

"I didn't know your sister lived on the wreck," Rani said.

"Oh, yes. Flora works there as a hairdresser," Octavius told her.

"Maybe we'll ask her to do our hair for the party," Rani's mother said, as she swam over to make sure they were ready. "Now, have you girls got your seaweed belts tied nice and tightly?"

Rani and Kai nodded. They each had a packed lunch tied to their belts, and a little purse containing the jewellery and hair decorations they were going to wear at the party.

"We'd better get going," said Murdoch.

"Bye-bye, Pearl," the girls said, rushing to give their baby sister a final hug. "We wish you were coming with us."

"Pearl will be just fine with me," Morva reassured them, as Pearl beamed happily at everybody from Morva's arms.

Just as they were leaving, Morva fastened a gold-coloured shell to Rani's belt. "The sea-spell is inside," Morva whispered. "And remember – it can only be used once, so don't use it unless you really have to!"

Rani promised that she wouldn't, as she gave Morva a goodbye hug.

They swam through the Deep Blue for a long time, with Murdoch leading the way. Rani and Kai swam behind him, with Octavius and Miriam swimming behind the girls. Every time Roscoe got tired he grabbed hold of one of the mermaids' hair and caught a ride with them for a while until he felt like swimming again.

The water in the Deep Blue was darker and colder than the water in

Tingle Reef. The further out they swam, the more strange the plants and rocks that surrounded them. Rani and Kai, who had never been this far out in the Deep Blue before, couldn't stop pointing things out to each other.

"Look!" gasped Kai, as a shoal of enormous fish swam by. Murdoch explained that a lot of the fish in the

Deep Blue were bigger than the ones they were used to seeing at home.

"Octavius, what have you *got* in those bags?" Kai asked the octopus, as they rested at the bottom of a large rock to eat their packed lunches. Murdoch was sitting on top of the rock acting as look-out.

"I have brought some of my famous stew for the party," Octavius said grandly, "since I know how much everyone likes it."

"Yes, but you don't eat *stew* at a party," Kai pointed out. "You eat mer-cakes and sea-trifle and—"

"What's that noise?" her mother interrupted.

There was a definite banging noise

that seemed to be coming from very close by.

"Murdoch!" Miriam called up to him, anxiously. "Can you come down here?"

"What's wrong?" Murdoch asked, swimming down to join them. Then he heard the noise too.

"There's a creature inside that rock. I can sense it," Rani said, frowning. Rani's magical powers often helped her to sense the presence of other creatures before they appeared.

Her family looked at her in disbelief. How could a creature be *inside* a rock? "I'm going to have a look," Rani said, swimming away from the others before they could stop her.

As she swam round to the other side

of the rock she noticed a bush growing out of it. The bush was swishing from side to side even though the water here was quite calm.

"Rani!" Her father appeared by her side just as a huge fish with sharp fins, a jagged tail, a huge mouth and very sharp teeth indeed, swam out from behind the bush.

"*SHARK!*" yelled Murdoch, pulling Rani behind him.

Rani started to fumble for the little golden shell that Morva had fastened to her belt – the shell with the sea-spell. But in her panic, the shell slipped from her fingers and floated away from her.

The huge shark was heading straight towards them, its white teeth flashing.

Then it seemed to sniff something it liked better. It batted Murdoch and Rani to one side and swam past them, heading straight for the others.

Rani and her father yelled out a warning, but it was too late. The shark had already trapped Miriam, Kai, Octavius and Roscoe. As they trembled against the rock face, the shark's evil black eyes glinted in pleasure at the prospect of such a yummy dinner.

That's when Rani heard the shark's thoughts floating towards her through the water. Rani's magic meant that she could often hear the thoughts of other sea creatures. The shark was smelling a mixture of mermaids and . . .

"Octavius! Throw him your stew!"

Rani shouted. "That's what he can smell!"

Octavius hastily untied his arms and pushed all the containers of stew towards the shark's open mouth. As the shark started to crunch it up greedily, Octavius and the others slipped past to join Murdoch and Rani.

"Quick!" said Murdoch urgently. "It won't take him long to get through that lot."

"Where's Rani going?" Kai asked suddenly.

Rani was swimming away from them, back towards the bush which had concealed the entrance to the shark's cave. "I have to get Morva's shell!" she called back. "You go on. I'll catch up with you in a minute!"

Rani spotted the shell straight away, gleaming up at her from a bunch of dark green seaweed. She picked it up and fastened it securely to her belt just as Murdoch caught up with her. He grabbed her firmly by the arm.

"I'm sorry, Father, but this shell is important," Rani said.

"So are you!" snapped her father. "Now, just *swim*! Before that shark realizes that the stew he's munching doesn't contain any mermaids at all!"

Chapter Three

"It's not far now," Miriam said, when Rani and Kai started to protest that they were getting tired. As they swam over a sandy opening in the rocks where lots of colourful fish darted about, Miriam became excited. "I recognize where we are! We're nearly there." She started to swim faster. "Look." She pointed ahead. "There it is!"

Rani and Kai looked ahead of them and couldn't believe what they were seeing. Even the descriptions their mother had given them hadn't prepared them for *this*.

Towering up from the seabed was the strangest structure they had ever seen. As they swam closer they saw that it was white because it was totally covered in limpet shells. There were many openings along the sides of the vessel – entrances to individual homes with colourful plants and flowers growing around the doorways. On top was a massive roof garden which stretched out over the whole area of the wreck. The garden was filled with all sorts of flowering shrubs and plants. Seaweed hammocks, strung up between the bushes, were swinging in the gentle current and there were lots of rock seats dotted here and there amongst the greenery. Some mermaids, who were relaxing in the garden, smiled and waved to them.

"It's beautiful!" gasped Kai and Rani together, as they waved back.

"Miriam!" someone called.

They turned to see an old mermaid with white hair swimming towards them.

"Mother!" cried Miriam, rushing forward.

The girls swam forward too, and soon their grandmother was hugging them tightly as she stroked their hair and told them how much they'd grown.

As everyone swam inside, Octavius asked about his sister Flora.

"She's very busy doing everyone's hair for the party tonight. Come with me and

I'll show you where we're having it."
Rani's grandmother led the way along
narrow corridors until they reached a
huge room with a tall ceiling and large
openings on both sides so that you could
see out into the Deep Blue in both
directions.

"It looks wonderful!" enthused
Miriam.

Rani thought it did too. A stone table along one side of the room was piled high with shell-dishes in readiness for the party. In one corner, a stage had been erected for the band. Purple and red seaweed decorations swung from the ceiling and the floor was sprinkled with glitter-sand.

"Hmm," murmured Octavius, who had swum up to inspect the ceiling and was now poking at it with the ends of his wriggly arms. "This ceiling is sagging."

"I don't see it," said Rani's grandmother sharply.

"Well, it is," said Octavius soberly. "You realize that if the ceiling collapsed, the whole roof garden would fall on top of us." He paused so that everyone could imagine being crushed by the roof garden, before adding, "Of course, I expect it's safe enough for the time being." He swam down to join them. "Now, I really must go and see my sister."

"Ask her if she'll do our hair too," Rani's mother called after him.

Octavius waved one arm at her to show that he would, as he swam off muttering under his breath. Really, it was hopeless trying to get mermaids to think about anything but their hair! They *meant* well, but they were such silly, scatty creatures. Still, he supposed it wasn't really their fault they had such tiny brains – unlike *his* which felt so heavy these days that he was beginning to

wonder if it was *growing*! He must ask
Flora what she thought. Now . . . where
was she? He couldn't wait to see the
surprise on her face when she saw him!

"You both look lovely," Rani's
grandmother said, as she watched her
two granddaughters get dressed up for
the party. "Now . . . I have a surprise for
you."

The girls gasped as she opened the lid
of an old wooden box to reveal all sorts
of necklaces and bracelets and rings.

"This is my treasure chest," said their
grandmother. "Whatever you choose
from it to wear tonight is yours to keep,
so choose carefully."

"Oh, Grandmother!" cried Rani, her

eyes shining with excitement. "They're all beautiful."

"Especially this," said Kai, picking out a necklace of aquamarine that matched her eyes. "May I *really* have it?"

Her grandmother nodded. "And what about you, Rani? What will you choose?"

Rani's gaze fell on a simple pendant made out of a large amber stone. She picked it up.

"Ah, the amber pendant . . ." said her grandmother. "I found that one day when I was out looking for some special plants to make up some medicines. It was just lying there on the seabed. And the same day, Pat, the dolphin arrived and told me that your mother and father

had found a baby that morning, inside
a Giant Clam-Shell."

"So we both got found on the same
day!" Rani said, carefully fastening the
pendant round her neck.

"It's glowing!" Kai gasped.

Rani looked down at the pendant.
The amber stone really did seem to be lit
from the inside now that it was touching
Rani's skin.

"Let me try it on," Kai said.

The girls swapped necklaces but for
some reason the pendant looked quite
dull and ordinary on Kai.

"I like mine better," said Kai, quickly
swapping back.

"Ah, here comes our hairdresser," said
their grandmother, as a loud jangling

noise attracted her attention.

Sure enough, the noise was Octavius's sister, Flora, who wore several bangles on each arm which clinked against each other as she moved about.

"Did Octavius find you?" Rani asked, excitedly. "I bet you weren't expecting him, were you? Did you get a lovely surprise when you saw him?"

"No, I certainly *wasn't* expecting him," said Flora, creasing her large forehead into a very wrinkly frown. "I've never been so—" She gave a polite cough as Octavius followed her into the room, ". . . so *surprised* in my life!"

"Nobody minds if I watch, do they?" Octavius asked, settling himself on the most comfortable-looking rock.

Since Flora had eight arms to work with, she could do marvellous things with mermaids' hair, very quickly indeed. Even Octavius was forced to admire the speed with which his sister combed and curled and crimped the long mermaid strands.

"If only I didn't have *red* hair," Rani sighed, as she waited for Flora to finish. Flora was using some of her arms as curlers in Kai's hair, so she only had three arms free to work on Rani. Octavius was suggesting ways his sister could use her arms even more efficiently as she wove Rani's hair into a long plait.

"I've only ever seen one other mermaid before who looked like you," Flora said, as she fixed Rani's shell-clasp

in place. "She had hair the same colour
as yours and she was very beautiful. She
told me she came from a secret place a
long way away."

"You're talking about Morva,"
Octavius interrupted impatiently. "We
all know her."

"This wasn't Morva," Flora said.

"Morva's ancient. This was a young mermaid. She had eyes just like yours, Rani, and she wore a pendant just like that one. She was resting in a cave because she was about to have a baby. Her husband had gone to look for food. I offered to do her hair for her. I couldn't resist – it was so beautiful."

"Where did you see her?" Rani gasped. "*When* was this? Did she tell you her name? Did she—"

"Oh, I can't remember the details," Flora interrupted. "It was about ten years ago. It was out in the Deep Blue somewhere."

"Flora – you've never told me any of this before!" Octavius said crossly. "This is very important information. How can

38

you forget to mention something like this?"

Flora started to jangle her bangles in an irritated manner. "I probably wasn't speaking to you at the time," she snapped back. "Since you were just as much of a know-all ten years ago as you are now!"

"Well, really," Octavius snorted, and the two octopuses started to bicker loudly.

Rani was stunned. Flora had met a red-haired mermaid with a pendant just like hers! And that mermaid had been about to have a baby – a baby who would be Rani's age by now! What if . . . What if . . . What if the mermaid Flora had met had been Rani's true mother?

chapter four

There was no time to ask Flora any
more questions because by the time she
had finished arguing with Octavius, it
was almost time for the party to begin.
But she promised to come and find Rani
later so they could talk some more.

As the mermaids gathered together in
the big hall, chattering excitedly, Rani
thought that they all looked beautiful.
Their long hair had been dressed up by
Flora and decorated with shell-combs
and flowers, and they all wore lovely

jewellery made from shells or precious stones. The mermen looked very handsome too, with garlands of twisted leaves on their heads and colourful seaweed belts.

The band was the biggest Rani had ever seen. Mermaids and mermen were playing shell-horns, flutes and drums of all different kinds. There was even a harp with bind-weed strings. But Rani's favourite thing was the glocken-shell – an instrument made up of lots of different-sized shells, each one sounding a different note when it was played.

Rani was scanning the room for Flora. Flora had said she was coming to the party too, when she had finished doing everyone's hair. Where was she?

"First, everyone must have a turn at singing," announced Rani's grandmother.

Mermaids were known for their beautiful voices and most of them loved to sing, but Rani had always felt far too shy to sing in front of other people.

Rani's mother sang first. She had a particularly lovely voice and everyone had tears in their eyes as they listened. Rani really wished that she could sing like that. As the other mermaids took their turns Rani started to feel nervous. She had to be the only mermaid whose voice always trembled whenever she tried to sing. What would the others think of her?

"Rani, it's your turn now!" her

grandmother said.

Rani was about to make an excuse when she happened to glance down at her pendant. It made her happy just to look at it and suddenly she felt like she could do anything if she really wanted to! She swam up on to the stage and – much to her amazement – found herself able to sing after all. In fact, she sang so beautifully that the whole room clapped and cheered when she had finished.

"I never knew you could sing like that," whispered Kai afterwards.

"Neither did I," gasped Rani, touching the pendant in awe. She was about to say more about it to Kai when their grandmother announced that it was time to have supper.

Rani and Kai swam to the table to choose what they wanted from the delicious spread of mer-cakes and sea-trifles and ocean-fruits. The grown-up mermaids were drinking lots of mer-wine and getting very merry indeed.

"This is yummy. Not a bit of seaweed in sight!" laughed Kai, who was always being told off for not eating her greens.

"And no stew either!" laughed Rani. Suddenly she spotted Flora across the other side of the room. "I'll be back in a minute," she told her sister.

"Wait, Rani! Where's your necklace?" asked Kai, seeing that it was gone from Rani's neck.

Rani looked down. "Oh, no! It must have fallen off."

At that moment, Rani was surrounded by a group of mermaids who demanded that she sing for them again. Rani protested that she had to find her necklace first, but the others were very excited and wouldn't take no for an answer.

"Don't be a spoilsport, Rani!" her grandmother called out from the other side of the room.

Rani didn't know what to do. She couldn't tell her grandmother that she had lost the necklace, but how else could she explain that she didn't want to sing without it?

"I'll look for it," offered Kai. "Give them one song and then come and help me. Don't worry. It's got to be here *somewhere*. It must be."

Reluctantly, Rani agreed but as she took her place on the stage again, she had a horrible thought. What if it was the pendant that had given her the ability to sing before? What if now – without it – she was just as hopeless as ever? Rani's throat felt tight. Her stomach started to churn. She was sure that her voice would come out totally shaky and everyone would laugh at her. She quickly mumbled something about a sore throat and left the stage.

"I *can't* sing without my pendant," she told Kai.

"Maybe it fell off when you went to get your food," Kai said.

They swam back over the top of the

long table and looked in between all the dishes but they couldn't see the necklace.

Rani felt like crying.

"Don't worry. You can share *my* necklace," Kai said, putting her arm round her sister. "Or maybe Grandma has another one you can have."

But Rani knew that the amber pendant was far too special to be replaced.

"I've *got* to find it," she told Kai.

And together, the two sisters started to search again.

Chapter Five

It was getting late and Rani was starting to feel sleepy. She still hadn't found her pendant although she and Kai had searched the whole room. She kept checking to make sure that the little shell containing the sea-spell was still fastened to her belt.

Flora seemed to have disappeared from the party. Rani was just giving up all hope of speaking to her again when she heard an unmistakable jangling sound right behind her.

49

"Flora," Rani gasped. "I've been looking for you everywhere!"

"I've been avoiding Octavius," Flora confided. "He's just so *bossy*. It's just as well I don't live in Tingle Reef or he'd drive me mad!"

"He drives us mad too sometimes," Rani grinned. "But we know he always *means* well!"

The party had livened up even more since Octavius had suggested they dance a few reels. The mermaids were swishing their tails as fast as they could in time to the music as they held hands and swung each other round. Octavius was dancing with eight mermaids at once and looking very pleased with himself.

"It's getting very noisy," Flora said. "I

hope we don't upset our neighbours."

"What neighbours?" asked Rani.

Suddenly, as if in answer to her question, an incredible bellow sounded.

"Oh dear," Flora said, looking out into the Deep Blue with a worried frown on her face.

"What is it?" asked Rani anxiously.

Flora pointed out into the dark water

which had suddenly become very choppy, and Rani saw an enormous black-and-white whale charging towards them.

"Whales have got very sensitive hearing," Flora whispered. "She's probably come to complain about the noise."

The furious whale banged against the side of the wreck and everyone stopped dancing.

The other mermaids made way for Rani's grandmother as she swam to the edge of the room so that she was looking out at the whale through a gap in the side of the wreck. "We're *terribly* sorry for disturbing you," she began, politely. "Can we make up for it by offering you some refreshments?" She looked across to the table where Octavius was helping himself to the last of the trifle. "We have lots of mer-wine and sea-fruits and—"

"I only eat plankton!" barked the whale rudely. "And I've had a bellyful of that on the way here!" She belched loudly.

"Of course, we'll stop the music—" Rani's grandmother tried again, but the whale interrupted her.

"You shouldn't have started it in the first place! I'm sick of you mermaids and your silly parties! You never think about anyone else but yourselves!" And she rammed her whole body against the side of the wreck again, in protest.

"The ceiling!" somebody yelled, as a

loud ripping noise came from above their heads and splinters of driftwood and barnacles started to fall from above.

The mermaids looked up and screamed. The huge wooden beams that made up the ceiling were splitting down the middle.

"What are we going to do?" gasped Flora, as everyone tried to swim away at once. "The roof garden will cave in on us."

Rani knew that there was no time to lose. She had to use the sea-spell. She took the golden shell from her belt and clasped it tightly in her hand, concentrating as hard as she could on starting up the magic. Gold dust began to trickle out from inside the shell – the spell was being released! Rani closed her eyes to help her focus better. When she opened them again, the water in the room was sparkling.

"What's happening?" someone cried out.

The whole room and its contents – except for the mermaids themselves – seemed to have frozen. A huge piece of ceiling had stopped in mid-water as it fell. A heavy rock from the roof garden, which had been about to fall on top of the band, was suspended in the water, not moving.

"Quick!" shouted Rani. "Everyone must swim out. Now!"

It took several minutes to clear the whole room so that only Rani was left.

A layer of sparkling water surrounded her as she closed her eyes again. Now, all she had to do was fix the ceiling and the roof garden would be saved. She remembered everything Morva had taught her and concentrated very hard on the spell.

Everyone cheered as the ceiling slipped back into place and the roof garden was restored.

Rani's grandmother leaned closer to Miriam as they waited for Rani to join them outside. She spoke very quietly so that no one else could hear. "I understand now what you mean about Rani," she whispered. "She is very special."

Miriam nodded. "I know."

"She may want to go and find her true home one day," the old mermaid added gently. "You realize that, don't you, my dear?"

Rani's mother didn't reply.

When she was sure that the spell had *really* worked, Rani swam outside to join the others. She knew that her mother and grandmother had been watching her very carefully, and now Miriam seemed quiet. "Mother, is something wrong?" she asked, swimming up to her. "You look sad."

"I'm fine, Rani," Miriam replied. "We all are . . . Thanks to you." And she pulled Rani close and gave her a very tight hug.

Suddenly, there was a big shout

behind them. It was Octavius, still clutching his bowl of trifle. "You mermaids really aren't very good at cooking," he muttered, fishing something hard and shiny out of it. And Rani saw that what Octavius was holding up – half covered in gooey trifle – was her amber pendant!

chapter Six

"Octopuses are very emotional, aren't they?" Kai said the following morning, as they waited for Octavius to finish saying goodbye to Flora. Having argued for most of the visit, the brother and sister were now embracing each other and getting horribly tangled up.

Rani had finally got the chance to speak to Flora on her own but she hadn't really discovered anything more about the mysterious red-haired mermaid. Flora was certain that her amber pendant had been the same kind as Rani's, though, and she had added that the young mermaid had been very sweet-natured. But apart from that Flora couldn't tell her anything else. She didn't know what had happened to the mermaid after she had left her – or to her baby.

Murdoch gently reminded everybody that they needed to set off.

"I can't wait to see Pearl again!" Kai said, as she waved goodbye to her grandmother.

"Me too," said Rani. "And Morva!" Rani was longing to tell Morva everything that had happened.

But the journey home seemed to take for ever. Roscoe was so tired that he kept falling asleep holding on to Miriam's hair.

"We're probably tired out from all that dancing," Murdoch said. "That's why it seems like it's taking longer. We'll stop and rest soon."

Rani turned to her mother and noticed something.

"Where's Roscoe?" she asked.

Roscoe was no longer attached to Miriam's hair – he had definitely been there the last time she'd looked – and he wasn't swimming along beside them either. In fact, he was nowhere in sight.

Everybody stopped swimming and started to call out Roscoe's name.

"He must have got lost," Murdoch said, frowning. "Come on. We'd better go back and look for him."

"I just hope he hasn't got himself eaten," Octavius said. "There was an extremely large fish back there. Did you see it?"

"Octavius, *please*," Miriam said.

"Sorry, sorry," muttered Octavius. "Of course, sea horses are very difficult to digest. That fish will probably just spit him straight out again if it's got any sense. Of course, fish *don't* have a lot of sense—"

"Octavius, *be quiet!*" Murdoch hissed. "I think I can hear something."

When the others listened they could hear the noise too. It sounded like someone shouting from a long way away.

"Come on," said Murdoch. "Stay

close to me."

They swam off in the direction of the sound. As they got nearer they could tell that it was definitely Roscoe.

"HELP!" Roscoe was shouting. "GET ME OUT OF HERE!"

"I hope he's not shouting from inside that fish's stomach," Octavius said gloomily.

"*OCTAVIUS!*" Miriam and Murdoch snapped at him together.

They swam on a little further and then they saw him.

"Oh no!" gasped Rani. The little sea horse was stuck in the middle of a gigantic silver web.

"Keep back, all of you!" Murdoch called out, sharply. "That's a Giant

Sea-Spider's web. That silver stuff is spider glue. If you touch it, you'll get stuck too."

"Father, what are we going to do?" Rani asked, starting to panic. Giant Sea-Spiders caught other creatures in their webs in order to eat them. Everyone knew that. And any spider with a web as big as this one had to have a very large appetite indeed.

"Find some rocks to throw at the web and we'll try to break it that way," Rani's father said. But he sounded very worried.

As the others began to collect rocks, Rani hovered beside the web. If only she hadn't used up the sea-spell. Surely there was *something* she could do. After all, she knew how to do a mending spell, didn't she? Surely a *breaking* spell couldn't be that different?

She closed her eyes and concentrated, holding out her hands so that they were just above the edge of the web. She focused as hard as she could on conjuring up a picture in her mind of the web breaking. Her belly button started to tingle and the tingling quickly spread up over the rest of her body and down her arms. Her fingertips felt hot. She opened her eyes and saw that golden sparks were jumping from her fingers to the web.

"Look at Rani!" Kai shouted.

For an instant the whole web sparkled. Then there was a sudden burst of golden

light, the web broke with a *ping* and
Roscoe was hurled straight into Rani's
arms.

"It's OK, Roscoe. You're safe now,"
Rani cried, hugging the trembling sea
horse.

The others were amazed. They knew
that Rani was learning to do magic but

none of them had ever seen her use it on her own before.

"You're just like Morva!" Kai stammered, looking at her sister in awe.

"Not quite," Rani laughed, pulling sticky bits of web out of her hair. "But I hope I will be, one day."

Just then, a large sea snake slithered over Rani's tail, followed by several babies. "Don't worry," the mother snake hissed. "We're not poisonous. But *she* is!" She flicked out her tongue to point at the huge, hairy, eight-legged creature crawling along the seabed towards them. "I'd get out of here if I was you!"

"SWIM!" commanded Murdoch, grabbing Kai and Rani and using his large, powerful tail to propel them at top speed through the water.

"Come back," shouted the sea-spider. "I won't eat you! I only put that web up because it looks pretty!"

"Do you think that's true?" Rani gasped, as they kept swimming.

"Somehow," Murdoch said, slowing down as they reached a safe distance away, "I didn't feel like taking her word for it."

"I have always thought that there is something quite *unnatural* about a creature with hairy legs," Octavius shuddered, waving his arms about in disgust.

"Come on," laughed Murdoch. "Let's go home."

chapter Seven

Morva was trying to sing Pearl to sleep
when they got home. She had tied some
shells to some seaweed ribbons and
made a beautiful shell-mobile which was
dangling from the ceiling above Pearl's
cradle. Pearl shrieked with excitement
when she saw her parents and sisters
again, and stretched out her chubby
arms to be picked up by Miriam.

After everyone had hugged each other,
Rani took Morva to one side.

"Morva, I've got so much to tell you!"

Rani began excitedly, but she stopped
when she saw the look on her friend's
face.

"Where did you get that?" Morva was
staring at the amber pendant around
Rani's neck as if she had just seen a
ghost.

"My grandmother gave it to me. It
was in her treasure chest. She gave a

necklace to Kai too. Look." She pointed to her sister who was swinging Pearl round and round, making her giggle. But Morva kept her eyes fixed on Rani.

"Rani, that is no ordinary stone—" Morva started to explain but, at that moment, Rani's mother called over to them.

"Morva, thank you so much for looking after Pearl. Would you like to stay and have supper with us?"

Morva shook her head, still looking dazed. "I must be getting back to my lobsters and my starfish. The poor things will be wondering where I am."

"But, Morva . . ." Rani began. "Tell me what's *wrong*."

"There's nothing *wrong*, Rani," Morva

said, as she swam towards the door.
"You've just given me a bit of a shock,
that's all. Come and see me tomorrow.
I'll explain everything then!"

As soon as she woke up the following
morning, Rani set off for Morva's cave.
Her mother made her have some
breakfast first, but she was too nervous to
eat more than a few mouthfuls.

Why had Morva looked so shocked
yesterday when she saw the pendant?
And what did she mean about it being
no ordinary stone?

When she arrived at the floating cave,
Morva was cooking breakfast on her hot-
rock stove. "So, Rani . . ." Morva turned
and smiled at her. "You have found your

message-stone. Or it has found you! It gave me quite a start yesterday, to see you with it." She swam over and touched Rani's amber pendant.

"*Message-stone?*" Rani frowned. She had never heard of such a thing.

Morva motioned for Rani to take off the necklace. As she took it from her, she said, "Look how it stops glowing when it leaves your skin. It is yours for certain!"

"Morva, what *is* a message-stone?" Rani demanded, getting impatient.

"A message-stone . . ." Morva explained slowly, "is a special stone that magic mermaids wear when they are separated from their families. That way they can always be sure that their loved ones are safe."

"I don't understand," Rani said. "How can a stone tell you that? And anyway, my family *is* safe. I've only just left them."

"I'm not talking about your family *here*," said Morva. "I mean your true family – the family you were separated from as a baby. If this is *your* message-stone . . . if you open it . . . you will see your true family inside."

"But how—" Rani gasped.

"A message-stone will always open for its true owner," Morva said, as she dropped it back into Rani's hand. "You must blow on it."

Rani lifted the amber stone up so that it was level with her face. She filled out her cheeks with air and blew.

"That's it," Morva said.

As they watched, the stone seemed to be glowing even brighter in Rani's hand. Gradually, its surface changed. Instead of being hard, it was becoming soft, like jelly.

"Look inside now," Morva urged her gently. "Go on. Don't be frightened."

Slowly, Rani lifted the stone up again and looked inside. It was like looking in through a window. Inside, she could see a merman, a mermaid and two babies. They all had red hair. The mermaid was young and beautiful and looked a bit like Rani. The merman was broad-shouldered and handsome.

"Is this . . . Are they . . . ?" Rani stammered, unable to say any more.

"This must be your family at the time you were separated from them," Morva whispered.

"But . . . but there are *two* babies!" Rani said hoarsely.

"I know. Watch carefully and see what happens next."

As she watched, Rani saw the two babies slowly changing before her eyes. "That's *me*," Rani gasped, as one of the babies grew into a little girl. At the same time, the other baby changed into a little boy with short red hair and twinkling goldy-brown eyes like Rani's.

"You must have a twin brother," Morva said.

Only the man and the woman didn't change. As Rani watched, they slowly faded away until they had completely disappeared.

"Where have they gone? What does it mean?" Rani cried out.

"It means," explained Morva gently, "that your real parents must have died when you were a baby. I'm sorry, Rani."

Rani swallowed. She had known for a long time that her true parents might be dead. But somehow actually *seeing* them and then watching them disappear like that made the fact that they were gone for ever seem a lot more real. She would never meet them now. She felt a tear roll down her cheek.

"Did you know them?" she asked Morva.

"I didn't recognize them, no," Morva

said. "But remember how old I am,
Rani. I left my home a long, long time
before you were born . . . probably
before your parents were born too."

Rani was silent.

"Your brother is still alive though,"
Morva added, trying to cheer her up.
"Imagine that! A twin brother!"

"He probably doesn't even know he

has a sister," said Rani sadly.

Morva smiled. "I wouldn't be so sure. How do you know that he hasn't got his own message-stone, with *you* inside it?"

"Do you really think so?" That thought made Rani feel better. She looked up at Morva. "I want you to take me to the place *you* come from – the magic place – so that I can find him."

"I *will* take you," Morva said. "But you must be patient, Rani. Your magic is not yet strong enough for you to make the journey."

"When will it be strong enough?" Rani demanded impatiently.

"Soon," Morva replied, smiling. "Very soon – I promise! And until then you can watch your brother growing up inside your pendant. Now, come on. It's time we practised another spell. How about I teach you how to turn my breakfast into enough to eat for two?"

Rani laughed. She had to admit that she *was* starting to feel a bit hungry.

Chapter Eight

The next day Octavius invited them all round for supper.

"What do you think of our new necklaces?" Kai asked Morva, who was looking especially colourful in a red and orange seaweed shawl.

"Very pretty indeed," Morva replied. Both Morva and Rani had thought it best if no one else knew about the message-stone yet, so they had agreed to keep it as a secret between the two of them.

Octavius had cooked his best stew and everyone complimented him on how delicious it was as they tucked in and listened to him telling Morva the story of the huge whale. "Of course, I warned everyone about that ceiling before the party started," he reminded them, not

for the first time. "I don't like to say 'I told you so' but really . . . If you mermaids would only listen to me instead of—"

Morva interrupted him. "I hear your *stew* saved the day as well, Octavius," she said, giving Rani a wink. "Tell us about that!"

"My stew? Ah, yes, my stew . . . It's a good job I had the idea of throwing that shark my stew," Octavius said. "Otherwise I don't know what would have become of us all."

"But it was *Rani* who told you to throw the stew," Kai pointed out.

"Rani? Ah, yes – Rani had the same idea as me," Octavius blustered. "I remember we both had the idea at the same time. Well done, Rani!"

"I'm just glad you brought that stew with you, Octavius," Rani said quickly. "Or I don't know what we'd have done." She turned to Morva. "I dropped the sea-spell, you see, so we couldn't use that."

"Well, it sounds as if you put my sea-spell to very good use in the end, Rani," Morva replied. "And then used some magic of your own on the journey home, I hear!"

"She saved my life!" Roscoe butted in. "If it wasn't for Rani—"

". . . you'd be digested by now!" Octavius finished for him.

The little sea horse shuddered.

"Let's make a toast," said Murdoch,

holding up his glass of mer-wine. "To Rani – our very own magic mermaid!"

"And the best sister anyone could have!" added Kai, grinning.

"So are you!" replied Rani, swimming over to give her sister a hug. "And you, Pearl!" she added, quickly kissing her baby sister who was sitting on Kai's lap.

"Rani *also* has the most beautiful singing voice," Octavius told Morva. "I was hoping that she would sing for us tonight."

"I don't *really* have a beautiful voice," Rani murmured, touching her pendant.

"What do you mean?" Morva asked.

"Rani reckons she can't sing unless she's wearing her amber pendant," Kai said. "That's what you said at the party, isn't it, Rani?"

"Well, that's just silly," Rani's parents exclaimed at once. "Whatever gave you that idea, Rani?"

"Well . . ." Rani began, wondering if she ought to explain after all about the pendant being magic, but Morva interrupted her.

"You know, I've seen you become a lot more confident lately, Rani," she said, thoughtfully. "Perhaps that's what's made the difference."

"Do you really think so?" asked Rani doubtfully.

"There's only one way to find out," Morva replied. "Give me the pendant."

Rani handed it to her.

"Now," Morva said, "*I'll* hold the pendant while *you* sing."

Rani stared at her in horror. "*No way!*"

"Come on, Rani," Morva said. "You couldn't have been that bad at singing before!"

"I sounded all croaky like a sea-frog," Rani replied.

Everyone laughed.

When the laughter had died down, Octavius cleared his throat loudly. "Of course, *I* could always sing if Rani doesn't want to. I'm told I have rather a splendid voice myself."

The others looked at each other in alarm.

"Why don't we *all* sing?" suggested Morva quickly.

So that's what they did. And as they sang, Rani heard her own voice, rising confident and clear above the others, and that was when she noticed that Morva was still holding her pendant.

Morva swam over to her. "Magic isn't the answer to everything, Rani," she whispered. "Don't ever forget that!"

And Rani promised that she wouldn't

as Morva dropped the message-stone, with her brother inside, back around her neck.